It's beginning to look a lot like Rex-mas.

written by Amy Fellner Dominy
& Nate Evans

illustrated by AG Ford

Los Angeles New York

For information address Disney • Hyperion, 125 West End Avenue, New York, New York 10023.

First Edition, September 2018
10 9 8 7 6 5 4 3 2 1
FAC-029191-18201
Printed in Malaysia

This book is set in Billy/Fontspring; GillSans/Monotype
Designed by Beth Meyers

Library of Congress Cataloging-in-Publication Data

Names: Dominy, Amy Fellner, author. • Evans, Nate, author. • Ford, AG, illustrator.
Title: Cookiesaurus Christmas / by Amy Fellner Dominy and Nate Evans ; illustrated by AG Ford.
Description: First edition. • Los Angeles ; New York : Disney-Hyperion, 2018.
• Summary: "Cookiesaurus Rex wants to be the special cookie on Santa's plate"—Provided by publisher.
Identifiers: LCCN 2016045026 • ISBN 9781484767450
Subjects: • CYAC: Cookies—Fiction. • Christmas—Fiction. • Humorous stories.
Classification: LCC PZ7.D71184 Ch 2018 • DDC [E]—dc23
LC record available at https://lccn.loc.gov/2016045026

Reinforced binding

Visit www.DisneyBooks.com

For the librarians who encouraged our love of reading,
and the teachers who inspired us to write.

—A.F.D. and N.E.

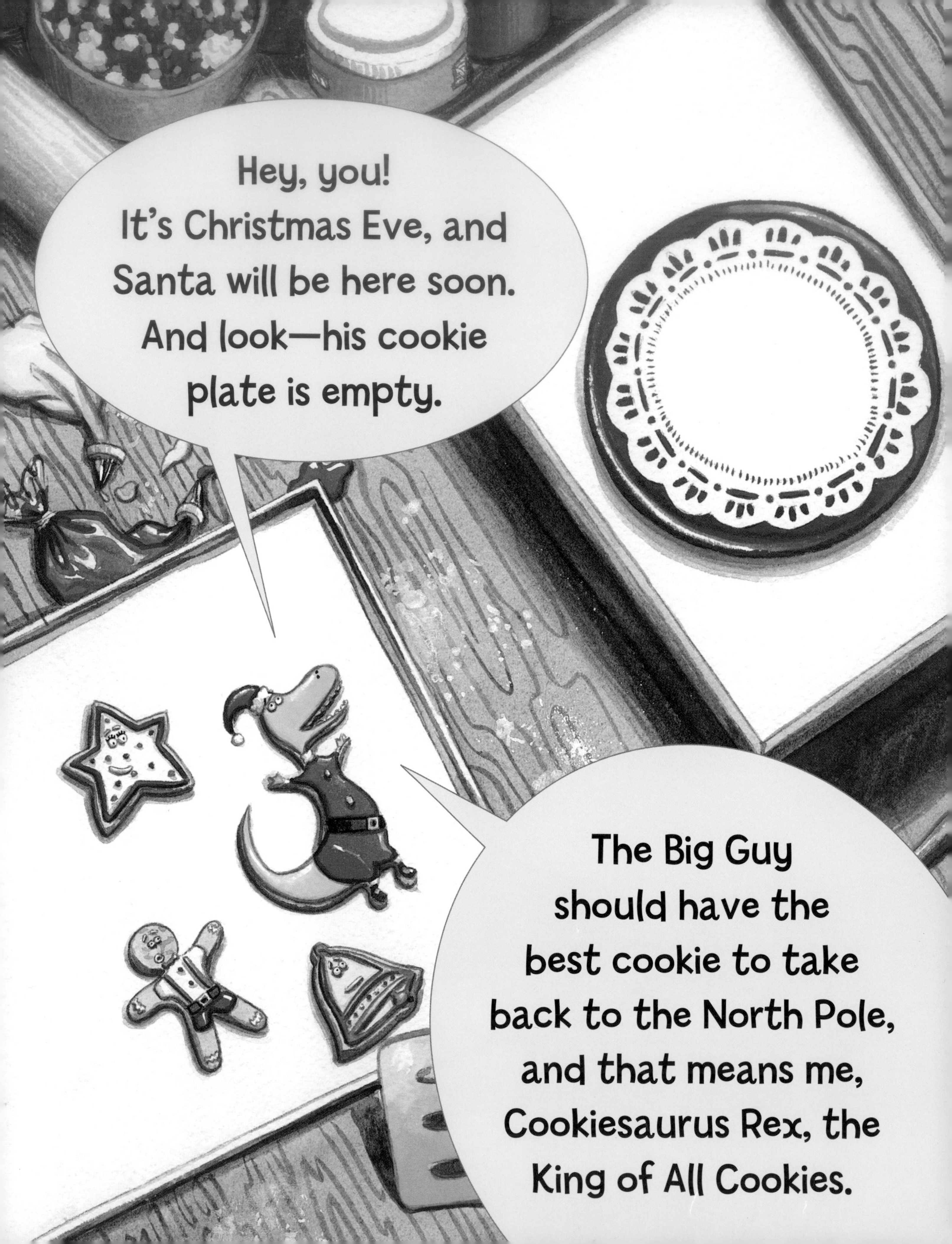
Hey, you!
It's Christmas Eve, and
Santa will be here soon.
And look—his cookie
plate is empty.
The Big Guy
should have the
best cookie to take
back to the North Pole,
and that means me,
Cookiesaurus Rex, the
King of All Cookies.

But does anyone think of dinosaurs at Christmas?
Is there a dinosaur on every Christmas tree? Are dinos hung by the chimney with care?
No! And it's not fair. Dinos have Christmas spirit too!

Me! Pick me! Come on, Mr. Spatula.

See what I mean?
What's so special about Star?
Is it because she twinkles?
Because I can tinkle too . . .
I mean TWINKLE!

Where are you going? Santa doesn't need a glass of milk. He needs another cookie. Like me!

If only I could fly . . . Wait! I can!

Oops.

Where did Star go? Uhhhh . . . maybe she was a shooting star? Good thing *I'm* here to save the day. Now you can give Santa a real present—ME!

No!
Don't put me back!
I want to be Santa's
cookie.

Bell gets to be the
lucky one?
You're picking that
ding-dong?

I’m coming over, Bell!

Yahooooo!

Double oops.

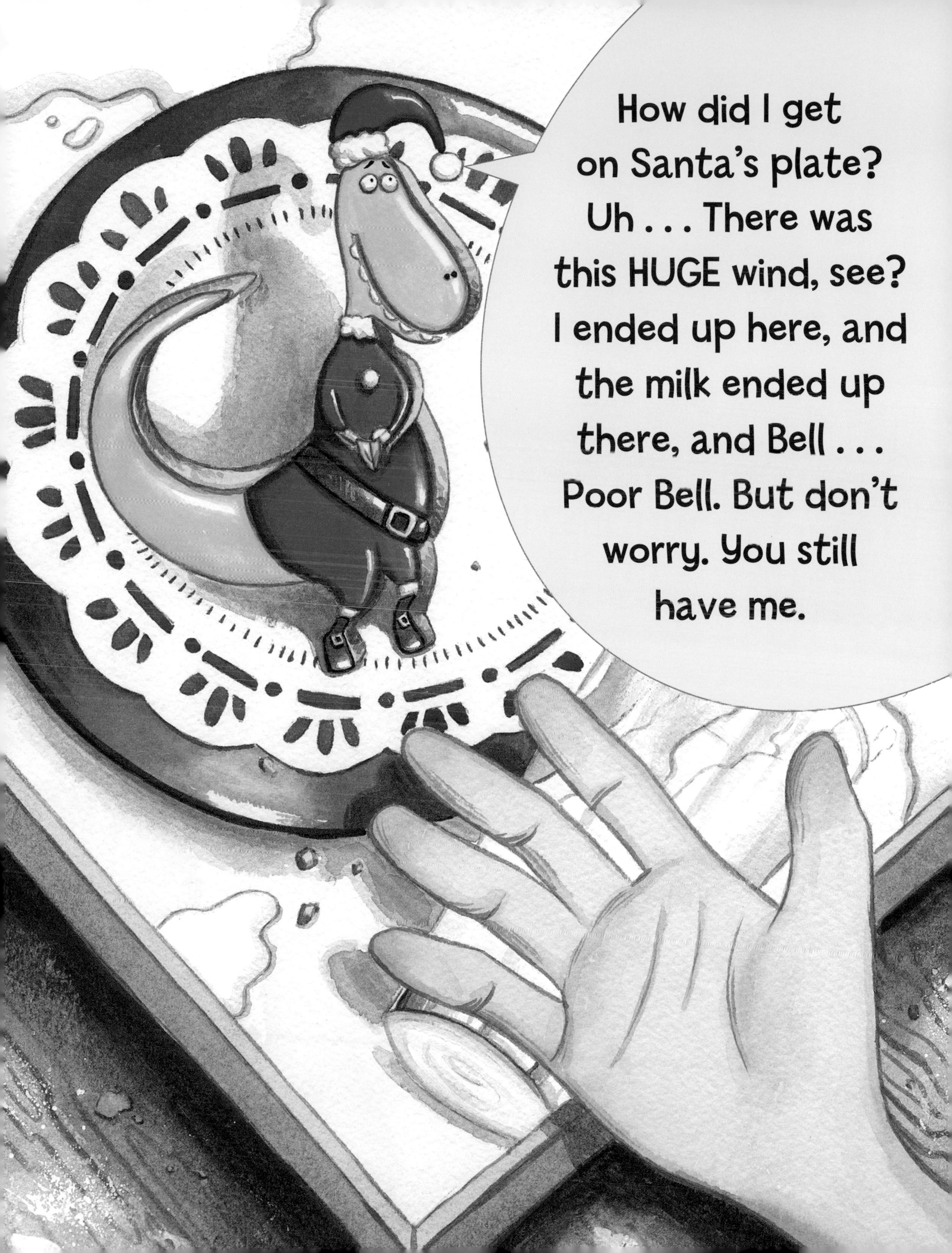
How did I get on Santa's plate? Uh . . . There was this HUGE wind, see? I ended up here, and the milk ended up there, and Bell . . . Poor Bell. But don't worry. You still have me.

Where are you going with me? You can't leave Santa's plate empty!

Wait one stinkin', stompin' minute!

Why can't it be me? I'm green, aren't I? And look, I have a mistle-*toe*. *I* should be Santa's cookie and get to ride on his sleigh and play reindeer games.

I'm making my move.
It's go time!

Catch me,
Gingerbread Boy!

Triple oops.

For Santa
There you are!
I don't know what happened
to Ginger. But look at Santa's
plate. It's still empty, and he'll
be here any minute!

Hello, Mr. Spatula.
Wheeeee, I'm flying!
It's really for real this time! I'm going to be Santa's cookie. North Pole, here I come!
Santa

For Santa
How do I look, guys? Guys? Buddies? Oh no. What have I done?

I'm a *crummy* cookie! Santa's going to put me at the top of his *Naughty List.* I only wanted to show that I had Christmas spirit too. I didn't mean to hurt anyone. It just sort of happened.

FoR
Santa

FoR
Santa

This is where you guys belong.
FoR
Santa

Don't worry about me.
I'll just be over here ALL alone.
No one wants a dinosaur
for Christmas.

Hey, where are
we going?

Oooh, it's sparkly in here. Are all those presents for ME?

Wait one stinkin', stompin' minute!

I'm on the Christmas tree? On the very TOP? This is . . . WOW! It's like . . . It's like I'm riding in Santa's sleigh! It's a Cookiesaurus Christmas!

Hey, Santa! Look at me— no hands!